Brigitte W...

Pictures by
Yusuke Yonezu

Bye-Bye
Binky

Translated by Kathryn Bishop

min⊜dition

Nori is a big boy now.
Nori doesn't need a pacifier anymore.
When Nori was little he called it Binky.
But when Nori is tired or sad,
he still puts it in his mouth.

One morning Binky fell out of Nori's pocket.
Ella Elephant found it behind the house.
"Too-too-too," she said happily.
"What a beautiful ring for my trunk."

Ella tried it on right away.
It looked very cute, but it was a bit tight.

So when she stopped for a drink of water
she took it off and left it by the pond.

Lotti Lamb found Binky by the edge of the pond.
"Baaaah," she said. "What a beautiful hair clip.
I can use this to keep these woolly bangs
out of my eyes."

Lotti tried on her new hair clip.
It looked very pretty, but it seemed a little loose.

As Lotti was enjoying her lunchtime grass
the clip slipped off her woolly head
and was left behind.

Henrietta Hen and her chicks,
One, Two and Three found the hair clip in the grass.
"Peep, peep," they exclaimed.
"What a wonderful swing!"

Henrietta hung the swing on a branch
and put One in it first.
Two also got to swing,
but Three fell down and started to cry.
So they left the silly swing there and went home.

Petey Pig found the swing hanging from the tree.
"Oink, Oink," he shouted.
"What a great thing.
This is perfect for my curly tail catapult!"

Petey tied the catapult onto his curly tail,
wound it up and let it go. BOING!
It flew over the roof and was gone.
"Oops…oh, well," thought Petey
and went on his way.

In the meantime, Nori was tired
and sad and wanted his Binky,
but he couldn't find it.
"We'll help you look for it,"
promised Ella, Lotti, and Petey.
Henrietta and One, Two and Three said they'd help too.

They found Binky behind the house.
"Too-too-too, there's the ring for my trunk," said Ella.
"Baa, baa, there's my hair clip," said Lotti.
"Peep, peep, peep, there's our swing," said Henrietta.
"Oink, oink, there's my curly tail catapult,"
said Petey.

Nori didn't say a word.

He picked up Binky and looked at it very carefully.
Then he said, "No, this WAS my pacifier.
But I'm big now, and I don't need it anymore."

And with that...
Nori let it go!
Bye-Bye, Binky.